Angel

in the
Wilderness

A Novella by

Majīd Pūr-Valī Kalashtarī

Translated by
Blake Archer Williams

Lantern Publications
info@lanternpublications.com
www.lanternpublications.com

Ordering Information:
Quantity sales. Special discounts are available on quantity purchases by corporations, associations, and others. For details, contact the distributor at the address below.

Shia Books Australia
www.shiabooks.com.au
info@shiabooks.com.au

ISBN 978-1-922583-45-1

First Edition

In the Name of God,
the Most Compassionate, the Most Merciful

1

Abdul-Hamīd took a last drag from his cigarette, threw the stub on the desert sand, and extinguished it with the tip of a worn shoe. He said, 'We're living in the 21st century. Clan and tribal arguments over creedal issues are absurd! When one can settle things through discourse, then one should do so; without any preconditions or excuses – with reason and rational proofs.'

He turned his head to face Hakīmeh-Khātūn, who was standing a few meters away by the side of the road in the harsh heat of the blazing sun. She was wearing a black chādor, and her gaze was fixed somewhere in the distance. Both sides of the narrow road were filled with an array of small and large sand hills, such that one could not see past them. The hills were covered with a fine, burnt khaki-colored sand which blew upward with the wind, which blew them into a whirling eddy. Abdul-Hamīd ran his hand over his white beard and said, 'The fact that you see four people gossiping in Bīrāh[1] is only because there has never been any precedent for such a thing before.'

Hakīmeh-Khātūn was holding her head down demurely and didn't respond. Abdul-Hamīd continued, 'So you're the first girl to have a Shī'a suitor.'

There were no cars to be seen on the road. The desert was calm and quiet; not a soul was to be found. Abdul-Hamīd raised his head and gazed skyward. No birds were to be seen in the sky either. Abdul-Hamīd looked at Hakīmeh-Khātūn again and said, 'The Shī'a are Muslim, like us. I have a few Shī'a friends in these very villages in Sīstān whom I've known for years. There is no enmity or rancor between us. They make their prayers in their own way, and I make mine. Their books say one thing, which is why they become Shī'a, and our books say something else, which is why we become Sunni. Our era is an era of Islamic unity. We must solve our problems united as brothers and in the spirit of friendship, and must put aside our differences.'

In order to get some kind of response out of Hakīmeh-Khātūn, Abdul-Hamīd asked her, 'What did you say his name was?'

Hakīmeh-Khātūn demurred from raising her head. Her gaze was still fixed on the hot desert sand. She looked at Abdul-Hamīd demurely with her head still lowered. Abdul-Hamīd was her senior uncle; a kind uncle who had taken the

---

[1] [The name of a village in Sīstān, in southeastern Iran. It literally means roadless.]

place of her father, for which Hakīmeh-Khātūn felt beholden to him. He father had died in a car accident on the Zābol road, after which Abdul-Hamīd had taken responsibility for her guardianship. Since the accident, Abdul-Hamīd had taken his brother's children into his own house and given them each an allowance and paid for all of their living expenses, even though he had four children of his own. He had taken on all of the responsibilities of fatherhood for them since that time. But today was one of those days in which Hakīmeh-Khātūn felt bashful, even before her Uncle Abdul-Hamīd.

She never thought there would come a day when she would want to introduce a young man to her family and say, 'This young man has asked for my hand in marriage!'

While still holding her head down, Hakīmeh-Khātūn said, 'His name is Rasūl. Rasūl Hedāyat.[2]

Abdul-Hamīd turned toward his pickup. He opened the passenger door and sat down slowly on the seat. There was a green kerchief around his neck, which he used to wipe the sweat from his brow. He looked at his wristwatch as he fanned himself to cool down.

'Its not far from Serāt to here. Two hours at most. Not more. He should have been here by now.'

Hakīmeh-Khātūn didn't say anything in response. She turned her head and looked at the horizon of the road.

---

[2] [In Persian (as well as in Arabic), Rasūl means messenger or apostle, and Hedāyat means guidance. But they are both common first and last names in Iran as well.]

Abdul-Hamīd asked, 'What does he do in Serāt? Does he have any family there? Where would we need to go to if we were to make inquiries about him? Who should we contact?'

Hakīmeh-Khātūn was doodling various patterns in the sand at the side of the road with the tip of her sneakers. Without turning to her uncle, she said, 'He's from Kermān, from Jayroft. But her sister was given in marriage to someone who lives in Serāt. And he now lives in Serāt, in his sister's house.'

Abdul-Hamīd nodded silently. He thought to himself, 'Whatever could prompt a Shī'a boy to come and ask for the hand of a Sunni girl in marriage? And in a place like Bīrāh, of all places – a village that is so out of the way and which doesn't have much to offer.' He reached down below his seat and retrieved a bottle of water. As he was uncapping it, he asked, 'Did he say anything when he realized you were Sunni?'

Hakīmeh-Khātūn shook her head slowly from side to side.

'No.'

Abdul-Hamīd took a sip of water and continued, 'So he didn't reconsider, or act as if he was having second thoughts?'

Hakīmeh-Khātūn said, 'I think he was taken aback a bit, but he didn't have second thoughts.'

Abdul-Hamīd nodded and said, 'Have you monitored him to see if he ever curses the *shaykhayn*?'[3]

---

[3] The 'two sheikhs'. The reference is to Abu Bakr and Umar, the first two caliphs, and the greatest of the Companions of the Prophet in the view of most Sunnis.

Hakīmeh-Khātūn said, 'He doesn't go in for that. He is always polite and even when he disagrees with something, he uses reasoned arguments.'

Abdul-Hamīd wiped his mouth and held the bottle of water out to Hakīmeh-Khātūn. 'Want some?'

He had discerned from her tone that she was fond of the Shī'a boy. And he knew that Hakīmeh-Khātūn was sober-headed when it came to these matters and didn't rush in to such decisions based on any initial emotional impulses. She wasn't like some of the girls whose hearts start to flutter and who lose all sense of themselves as soon as they go to university and see a few young men. Hakīmeh-Khātūn had had many suitors already, two of whom were engineers. But she had rejected them all. Maybe it was because she was a university student, or maybe it had some other reason that was unknown to Abdul-Hamīd, but now she had suddenly come and said, 'A Shī'a boy wants to come and ask for my hand in marriage!'

Hakīmeh-Khātūn glanced at the bottle her uncle was holding out and said, 'I'm not thirsty.'

She was very thirsty. She was so anxious that her lips were parched. Her mind was completely preoccupied with Rasūl. She kept thinking, 'What if he's late? What if he doesn't show up?'

She was worried about his not showing up, but she was even more worried about what would happen in their village if he *did* show up. She had asked her mother why he needed to come to Bīrāh, and her mother had responded, 'I want to see him! He'll come if he loves you.'

Abdul-Hamīd was still holding the bottle of water. Hakīmeh-Khātūn couldn't drink from a bottle which her uncle had drank from. Abdul-Hamīd glanced at Hakīmeh-Khātūn and returned the bottle to below the seat. He then leaned back on the pickup's faded seatback, looked out of the dust covered windscreen, and said, 'You are no longer a child, so I don't need to tell you what to do. After Ibrāhīm died, God rest his soul, I had to take on the responsibility for all of your affairs. And praise be to God, neither your mother nor any of your brothers disagreed with any of my decisions. Marriage is not a small matter. I have not been to university, as you have, but I have been a history teacher in these schools for thirty years. I've tasted the bitterness as well as life's sweetness. But I have yet to give away a daughter to a suitor, let alone to a Shī'a boy from some unknown place.'

He looked at Hakīmeh-Khātūn and continued, 'I can't say anything until I see him personally and understand what he really believes. I don't want to give you away to some uneducated idiot, be he Sunni or Shī'a.'

Without raising her head, Hakīmeh-Khātūn said very softly, 'He's not uneducated, *Amū Jān* (Dear Uncle). He's been studying at the university for three years already.'

Abdul-Hamīd nodded his head and said, 'I'm not concerned about whether anyone has or has not gone to college. There are university professors who don't even believe in God! My concern is with the Quran, and with God and His prophet. Who knows, he might even become Sunni like us after having lived alongside us for a couple of years.'

He stuck his head out of his pickup and said, 'Have you ever asked him about the *sahaba*[4]? About the Mother of the Faithful Āisha? He's going to be living among our brothers and sisters and the whole family for a whole lifetime. You need to know what passes through his head.'

Hakīmeh-Khātūn nodded and said, 'I've asked him.'

Abdul-Hamīd looked at Hakīmeh-Khātūn's face and asked, 'You mean you've asked him about the *sahāba* and Āisha??'

'Yes.'

Abdul-Hamīd looked at Hakīmeh-Khātūn in surprise and asked, 'Well, what did he say?'

'He said that he liked and approved of anyone whom the Prophet liked and approved of. He said that his criterion for liking or disliking anyone was the Quran and God's Apostle.'

Abdul-Hamīd nodded and said, 'That's good; the Quran is good.'

Suddenly it seemed as if Abdul-Hamīd noticed something in the distance. He climbed out of his pickup and stood at the side of the road looking at the horizon. A small dot was moving towards them from the distance. Abdul-Hamīd went towards Hakīmeh-Khātūn and said, 'I think that's him.'

He pointed to the horizon. Hakīmeh-Khātūn's heart began to beat faster. She turned her head towards the road. The moving dot grew larger and gradually took on the shape of a motorcycle. Rasūl was riding the motorcycle and

---

[4] [The Companions of the Prophet.]

approaching at speed. He reduced his speed as he came up to Abdul-Hamīd's pickup, and came to a stop. He approached Abdul-Hamīd respectfully and with a smile no his face.

'*Salām.*'

He extended a hand to Abdul-Hamīd, and they shook hands. Abdul-Hamīd was monitoring Rasūl's every move. Hakīmeh-Khātūn was standing at a distance and didn't approach them. Her *hayā* (rightful modesty) prevented her from doing so. She gave a nod to Rasūl from where she was standing in response to the quick glance that Rasūl had given her, and the *salām alaykum* that followed.

Abdul-Hamīd looked at Rasūl's bloodied sleeve in surprise and asked, 'What happened to your hand?'

Rasūl gave a bitter smile and strove to hide his left hand. 'It's nothing. I had a fall is all.'

Hakīmeh-Khātūn looked at Rasūl with concern. She wanted to perhaps go up to Rasūl and examine his hand, but couldn't do so with Abdul-Hamīd present, so she just looked at him with concern from afar.

Rasūl said, 'There was a large pothole in the road. I was going fast and before I knew it, the front wheel sank into it.'

Abdul-Hamīd rolled up Rasūl's sleeve and looked at the wound. 'It doesn't look good at all.'

He turned towards Hakīmeh-Khātūn. 'Hakīmeh, bring that yellow bag over, will you? It's behind the seat.'

A few minutes passed while Abdul-Hamīd cleansed Rasūl's wound with the water from the bottle and bandaged it with some gauze. A hot breeze passed across Rasūl's face as he sat on the pickup's passenger seat. It was as if he was sitting in front of a large bread-oven, and his face was being accosted by a plume of its fire.

Rasūl gave Abdul-Hamīd a smile and said with satisfaction, 'Thank you. It feels much better already.'

Abdul-Hamīd nodded, then asked, 'How old are you?'

'Twenty-Four.'

Abdul-Hamīd pointed to the road before them and said, 'This is the road to Bīrāh. This is the road we're going to take. Its about an hour's drive.'

Rasūl looked at the road. 'Why have they named it Bīrāh?'

He looked at Abdul-Hamīd, who was washing his hands with the rest of the large bottle of water. Abdul-Hamīd replied, 'Because it was out in the middle of nowhere for a very long time. Somewhere no one ever had occasion to visit. Nor was there a road that led to it.'

Rasūl got out and stood up and lowered his sleeve. He looked at his motorcycle and said, 'So take the lead, and I will follow you.'

Abdul-Hamīd gave him a rueful smile. 'Are you afraid to ride with us?'

Rasūl responded in surprise, 'No.'

Abdul-Hamīd chuckled. 'I think you're a little intimidated. Otherwise, you'd ride with us in the pickup.'

Rasūl gave a quick glance to Hakīmeh-Khātūn and said, 'I'm not scared. I just...'

He didn't finish his thought. He wanted to say that he didn't want to ride in the pickup because it would not be appropriate for him and Hakīmeh-Khātūn to ride so close to each other [where their bodies would touch] in the pickup.

Abdul-Hamīd said, 'Come and help me load your motorcycle into the back of the pickup.'

The two of them managed with some difficulty to load the motorcycle up onto the tailgate and into the bed of the pickup. Abdul-Hamīd indicated to Hakīmeh-Khātūn, saying, 'Ride in the back.'

Rasūl looked at her with misgiving, but demurred from saying anything. He didn't want Hakīmeh-Khātūn to sit in the back of the pickup in the blazing sun for an hour. He looked at Abdul-Hamīd and asked with some trepidation, 'Would it be alright for me to ride in the back instead?'

Abdul-Hamīd looked at him in bewilderment. 'Then who would I speak to if you sat in the back?'

Rasūl said nothing. Hakīmeh-Khātūn climbed into the back of the pickup, and Abdul-Hamīd and Rasūl sat in the front, and they were off.

2

They had not traveled far before Rasūl spoke up, saying, 'If it'd be alright with you, I'd like to return to Serāt before sunset.'

Abdul-Hamīd had his mind on the road. 'Return? So soon?'

Rasūl smiled and said, 'Tomorrow is a religious holiday, and there is still a lot of preparation work to do that I need to help out with.'

Abdul-Hamīd looked at Rasūl and asked, 'What holiday is that?'

'Eid al-Ghadīr.'

Rasūl had his eyes on the road, which extended into nothing but the wilderness of the desert. The level of the sand dunes moved up and down as they passed them. Occasionally a few small palm trees could be seen between them, and these disappeared in the blink of an eye, being replaced with an endless sea of sand. But the sky above their heads was a deep blue; it seemed to Rasūl that he had never seen such a deep blue in the sky before. Hakīmeh-Khātūn had talked to him about the desert sky on numerous occasions. Rasūl had seen deserts before, but it seemed as if the desert of these parts harbored a special sense of homesickness and forlornness in its sand dunes. There were hardly any trees, and there was no vegetation, just sand and nothing else.

'But wasn't Eid al-Ghadīr yesterday?'

Rasūl said, 'As a history teacher, you should know that it took the community three whole days to be able to pledge allegiance to Amīr al-Mu'minīn [the Commander of the Truly Faithful; reference to Imam Ali] after the Prophet delivered his farewell sermon at al-Ghadīr.

Abdul-Hamīd nodded but said nothing. It seemed he might not have appreciated Rasūl's tone. Nor was he pleased that Hakīmeh-Khātūn had told Rasūl that he was a history teacher. He glanced at Rasūl and said with a smile, 'So why do you say "Amīr al-Mu'minīn"? Why don't you just say Imam Ali? Like us. That's what we say: "Imam Ali". Or like how you say "Imam Hasan" or "Imam Husain" or "Imam Riḍā".

Rasūl's eyes were on the road. He replied, 'We have been commanded to say Amīr al-Mu'minīn, and so we obey and refer to Imam Ali as Amīr al-Mu'minīn. He is the only Imam out of the Twelve concerning whom we use this appellation, which has been bestowed upon the Imam by God; all we are doing is obeying His command.'

Abdul-Hamīd gave a surprised look at Rasūl and said, 'But I haven't heard of any such commandment.'

Rasūl said, 'It has probably passed your notice, because this matter also appears in your sources.[5] It is reported in hadith reports that the Prophet has said that whenever you want to address Ali, you should do so by referring to him as Amīr al-Mu'minīn, and that this is an honorific that God has designated for Ali.'

Abdul-Hamīd replied, 'There were all these Abbāsid caliphs who were referred to as Amīr al-Mu'minīn. You can't deny that, can you?'

Rasūl said, 'Those caliphs placed this label on themselves. It is not as if they commanded the loyalty of the faithful. It's just like an unjust king ordering his subjects to refer to him as "So-and-so the Just". Rather, the title Amīr al-Mu'minīn's true value is due to the fact that it was bestowed by God on a human being. And the only person God has made such a bestowal in favor of from the prophet Adam to the last person to walk the earth is Imam Ali.'

Rasūl then looked at Abdul-Hamīd and said, 'There is actually another hadith report, whose exact wording escapes me right now, which talks about people who falsely appropriate this title for themselves.'

Two women could be seen in the distance now, walking in the same direction as the pickup. Abdul-Hamīd reduced his speed and slowed to a stop next to them. The women turned around, and seeing who it was, greeted Abdul-Hamīd warmly, after

---

[5] It has been related by the Sunni scholar Abū-Na'īm al-Isfahānī in his *Hilyat al-Awliyā'* from Anas ibn al-Mālik. The hadith report also appears in Ibn Mardūya al-Isfahānī's book.

which they looked at Rasūl and exchanged some words with each other. Abdul-Hamīd offered to give them a lift, after which they climbed into the back of the pickup with Hakīmeh-Khātūn.

When they started off again, Abdul-Hamīd said, 'Did you notice the older woman?'

Rasūl looked at Abdul-Hamīd and said, 'I didn't pay much attention.'

Abdul-Hamīd said, 'Her name is Rābi'a. Her son Adnān is Hakīmeh-Khātūn's suitor. This same woman has sent more than ten messages to me asking for permission to come and ask for her hand in marriage for her son.'

Abdul-Hamīd looked at Rasūl's face to see his reaction. Rasūl continued to stare at the road in silence.

Abdul-Hamīd said, 'Don't you have anything to say about that?'

Without looking at him, Rasūl said, 'What am I supposed to say?'

That didn't sit well with Abdul-Hamīd, who shook his head and said, 'That's it? "What am I supposed to say."?!'

Rasūl turned his head towards Abdul-Hamīd slowly. He tried to smile so as to show Abdul-Hamīd his equanimity. He said, 'Probably Hakīmeh-Khātūn has not agreed to such a union, which is why you have not given your permission.'

Abdul-Hamīd said, 'Adnān is about your age. He has a job, a house, and a car. He is tall, and is not blind or lame or even bald! And he is a very good boy, with a strong faith in God.'

Rasūl looked at Abdul-Hamīd with surprise. He still didn't understand why he was saying these things. Was this, perhaps, his way of showing his disagreement with the proposed union from the start? But if that was the case, why did he have Rasūl ride with him in the front, and why was he taking him to Bīrāh at all? He could have just told him right there where they met that he was not amenable to such a union, thereby putting an end to everything.

Abdul-Hamīd kept his eyes on the road and continued, 'My point isn't about what Adnān has and what you don't have. What I'm saying something else. Something that is more important than all of that.'

He turned his head back and glanced at the two women and Hakīmeh-Khātūn, then continued, 'Tell me, what am I supposed to say if these women and all of the people of Bīrāh ask me why I didn't give Hakīmeh-Khātūn's hand in marriage to Adnān, who is from the same village and has the same creed as we do, rather than gaving her to one who is both a stranger and whose creed is different from ours?'

He stared into Rasūl's face. 'From the time Hakīmeh-Khātūn told me and her mother about you, I have constantly asked myself what *possible* reason there could be for me to agree to your and Hakīmeh-Khātūn's marriage. No matter how much I think about it, I can't come up with an answer to this question. Now let me ask you a question: tell me, with all the Shī'a girls that are available, why have you come after Hakīmeh-Khātūn?'

He looked at Rasūl and waited for an answer. Rasūl just smiled a bitter smile and said nothing. He didn't know how he was supposed to respond. Perhaps if Abdul-Hamīd was smart and more observant, he would have seen from the vacillation of Rasūl's pupils that a larger secret was afoot. A larger secret which Rasūl dared not mention. A big secret which had compelled Rasūl to come to Serāt from Jīroft, and to come from Serāt to Bīrāh by himself and with no one else; a secret for whose revelation an opportunity might not arise, and which might remain and be buried right there in Rasūl's heart. Abdul-Hamīd glanced at his watch and stepped on the gas. He wanted to get to Bīrāh in time for the noon prayers.

He glanced at Rasūl and said, 'As you said, I'm a history teacher. The study of history has instilled reason and rationality in me. I am guided by rational arguments and proofs. Hakīmeh-Khātūn told me that you are a young man who is well versed in rational arguments and proofs. If this is really the case and Hakīmeh-Khātūn has spoken the truth and has evaluated you aright, then tell me, if you were in my place, what would you do?'

Rasūl looked at him with surprise and said, 'If I were in your place?'

Abdul-Hamīd nodded his head and said, 'Yes. Imagine you are in my place and Hakīmeh-Khātūn is your daughter. Imagine that in your creed and belief system, Abū Bakr and Umar and Uthmān and Mu'āwiya and Āisha and Talha and Zubayr and all of the Companions of the Prophet are honorable people whose memory is sacred. Then one day, a suitor comes along whose beliefs are different than your own and asks for the hand of your daughter in marriage. What would you do? Would you be willing to give your daughter away to him?'

It seemed for a moment as though Rasūl had been taken by surprise. He then shook his head, smiled, and said, 'No!'

Abdul-Hamīd laughed and said, 'What do you mean, "No"?? Explain yourself!'

Rasūl said, 'I would not be willing to give my daughter to anyone who did not hold the same beliefs as I do.'

Abdul-Hamīd let out a loud peal of victorious laughter, then nodded his head and placed his hand on Rasūl's shoulder and said, 'Excellent! I congratulate you on your sincerity! I like the fact that you are independently minded. Now *that* was a rational response! Fully grounded in reason.'

With that, Abdul-Hamīd brought his attention back on the road, but he now had a big smile on his face. He was happy that he had been able to make Rasūl admit that he had taken the wrong path. That was half the battle: to make Rasūl reconsider his request. After that, making Hakīmeh-Khātūn change her mind would not be that difficult. He knew that Hakīmeh-Khātūn was not given to stubbornness and fiery bouts of love and taking the position of "either death or marriage" to a particular person. She could be persuaded to see reason with just an hour's worth of rational argumentation. She was the kind of girl for whom hours of speeches and sermons and worthless advice had no effect, but for whom a single well-reasoned sentence would calm down and make her abide. Maybe that is why she had taken a liking to this young Shī'a man. A young man who it seemed had been suddenly disarmed by Abdul-Hamīd. Rasūl was staring out of the windshield into the barren wilderness. Abdul-Hamīd didn't want to leave him to wallow in his misery. He felt sorry for the lad.

He said to himself, 'The poor young man has come all this way with a whole bunch of love in his heart. It would not be pleasing to God for me to upset him like this.'

He smiled at Rasūl and asked, 'Have you ever been in these parts before?'

Rasūl shook his head and said, 'No.'

Abdul-Hamīd's attention was on the road. He said, 'Then you haven't seen the woods of Harrā yet!'

He glanced at Rasūl. 'Have you tasted the tropical fruit here?'

'No.'

'Then you don't know what you're missing!' Abdul-Hamīd chuckled and continued, 'The soil of these parts is fecund. Sometimes one sees some plants and creatures in this very wilderness that you wouldn't believe. My father has seen black bears and leopards here!'

Abdul-Hamīd smiled at Rasūl. 'Can you believe it? Leopards!'

He focused on the road again. 'Alligators have been seen here too.'

He shook his head ruefully. Rasūl saw that Abdul-Hamīd was shaking his head. Abdul-Hamīd let out a loud moan of remorse and said, 'But all that aside, we do not have any drinking water here. You might not believe it, but there is a village not far from here where the people have to walk four kilometers for water.'

He chuckled again, then said, 'You've gone all quiet. Everything OK?'

Rasūl smiled a bitter smile and said, 'Yeah, fine. I was thinking about your question.'

Abdul-Hamīd nodded his head and said, 'Like I said, I've studied history! I'm not your run-of-the-mill uneducated person. I like reasoned arguments. I will accept any well-reasoned argument, no matter who it comes from.'

Rasūl said nothing. He was still looking ahead into the wilderness and the desert sand. Abdul-Hamīd was keeping an eye on the road with one eye, and sneaking glances at Rasūl with the corner of the other.

He said, 'So what are you thinking of now that is so deep and heavy?'

Rasūl said, 'I was thinking of the Apostle of God.'

'The Apostle of God?'

'Yes. I see now more than ever how right he was, with what you just said.'

Abdul-Hamīd, who had no idea what Rasūl was talking about, said, 'What are you talking about? I was talking about you and Hakīmeh-Khātūn; what does that have to do with the Apostle of God?'

Rasūl looked at Abdul-Hamīd and said, 'Many suitors asked the Prophet for Lady Fātima's hand in marriage too. As one who has studied history, you should know that the first caliph and the second caliph were among those suitors.'

Abdul-Hamīd nodded and said, 'Yes, so I have read.'

Rasūl said, 'But the Prophet of God did not give her daughter to those two suitors. Ultimately, Lady Fātima married Imam Ali. Maybe that was because the Prophet wanted to give his daughter away to one who had the same beliefs and disposition that he himself had. And he didn't want to have a groom who did not share his creed and worldview.'

Abdul-Hamīd did not expect to hear anything like this. He became indignant and said, 'What does any of this have to do with what we were talking about?'

Rasūl said, 'There is a hadith report that states that the husband of Lady Fātima was chosen by God himself. In other words, it was God who in fact rejected all those who came to the Prophet to ask for Lady Fātima's hand in marriage. And when Imam Ali was chosen, this choice was in fact God's choice.'

Abdul-Hamīd nodded but didn't say anything. He was not enamored by Rasūl's always having answers at the ready. But on the other hand, what Rasūl had to say was not something that could be easily dismissed. Abdul-Hamīd said to himself, 'Why hadn't I thought of this before myself?'

He thought, Hmm, why shouldn't the Prophet give his daughter in marriage to either of the first two caliphs?? What was wrong with them that prevented him from doing so? The fact that the first two caliphs were indeed suitors for Lady Fātima, and that they had been turned down, was not something that could be passed over or concealed, as reports of these events appeared in all of the authoritative history books. Furthermore, if what this young man was saying is true and that it was God was who chose Lady Fātima's husband, one must determine why it was that He did not want either of the first two caliphs to be joined in wedlock with her.

Abdul-Hamīd spent the next few minutes thinking about this, and realized that he didn't have an answer to these questions. He decided that he needed to study the issue further.

Rasūl tilted his head to his left to get a different view of the sky, then said, 'It seems it's going to rain.'

Abdul-Hamīd looked at the sky and smiled and said, 'Rain? *Here?*' He then turned to look at Rasūl, then continued, 'It's been nearly seventy years since Bīrāh has seen any rain. If you said it was going to rain stones, I would believe you; but rain? Never.'

He fixed his gaze on the road. Gradually, small outcroppings of desert vegetation could be seen every once in a while. Rasūl looked at the scrawny bushes as they passed them by. They were covered in a fine mist of dust.

Abdul-Hamīd continued the conversation. 'I don't talk much with Shī'a Muslims. What I mean is that I don't go in for arguments and debates and that kind of thing. I prefer tranquility. I'm the kind of person who prefers to set aside our differences. I'm more inclined to friendship and fellowship and brotherhood. Nor do I have any truck with the past. The past is past. Rather, we must think of the future. And with respect to ourselves and the Shī'a, I believe that we should only promulgate unity between us. I support the notion of Islamic unity; I support the unification of the Muslim community. I think that if Islam is to achieve a desirable objective, it can only do so through Islamic unity.'

Rasūl nodded and said, 'I agree with you.'

Abdul-Hamīd looked at him with great surprise and asked, 'You agree? I doubt you are telling the truth!' He chuckled as he said this.

Rasūl asked in surprise, 'Why do you say that I'm not telling the truth?'

'Because from the very first moment that you got in the truck you've been talking about Imam Ali!'

Rasūl said, 'That's because Imam Ali just so happens to be the main pillar upon which this unity can be erected!'

Abdul-Hamīd looked at him in bewilderment and asked, 'What does Imam Ali have to do with Islamic unity??'

Rasūl said, 'On the day that the Prophet delivered his Farewell Sermon at Ghadīr Khumm, he raised Ali's hand, indicating him to the multitude of Muslims as being the main pillar of the unity of the *umma* (purposive community, or community with a uniformity of purpose). The Prophet raised Ali's hand in order to make people understand that Ali and only Ali is the pillar upon which Islamic unity can be erected.' Rasūl then paused for emphasis, then continued, 'Ask yourself why the Prophet did not raise the hand of some of the other Companions alongside Ali, and chose only to raise his hand? Go and study our history in detail and see which of the Companions started to talk out loud in the middle of the Prophet's sermon that day in order to sabotage his message. Go and see which ones wanted to assassinate him for declaring this choice openly and publicly!'

Abdul-Hamīd shook his head and said, 'Ghadīr has nothing to do with Islamic unity.'

Rasūl said, 'Yes, it does. They are definitely related. And the Quran so.'

The mention of the Quran made Abdul-Hamīd turn and look at Rasūl. 'The Quran??'

'Yes, the Quran.'

'What does the Quran have to say about this?'

'The Quran says, [3:103] *And hold fast, all together, unto God's bond, and do not draw apart from one another.* And what is this *God's bond* which God has asked us to hold onto so that we do not *draw apart from one another*? It is stated in both Sunni as well as Shī'a commentaries that what is meant by *God's bond* is Imam Ali.[6]

وَاعْتَصِمُوا بِحَبْلِ اللَّهِ جَمِيعًا وَلَا تَفَرَّقُوا ۚ وَاذْكُرُوا نِعْمَتَ اللَّهِ عَلَيْكُمْ إِذْ كُنتُمْ أَعْدَاءً فَأَلَّفَ بَيْنَ قُلُوبِكُم فَأَصْبَحْتُم بِنِعْمَتِهِ إِخْوَانًا وَكُنتُمْ عَلَىٰ شَفَا حُفْرَةٍ مِّنَ النَّارِ فَأَنقَذَكُم مِّنْهَا ۗ كَذَٰلِكَ يُبَيِّنُ اللَّهُ لَكُمْ آيَاتِهِ لَعَلَّكُمْ تَهْتَدُونَ ﴿١٠٣﴾

[3:103] And hold fast, all together, unto the bond with God, and do not draw apart from one another...

Abdul-Hamīd said with surprise, 'I have not read or heard anything to this effect.'

---

[6] See, for example, the *tafāsīr* of Tha'labi, *al-Manāqib al-Fākhira*, and not least, [the hadith with] the provenance title of Muhammad b. Abd-Allāh b. Mu'ammar al-Tabarāni, who was a friend of Yazīd b. Mu'āwiya.

Rasūl said, 'The criterion of something being true is not, of course, whether you or I have or have not read or heard about it. One is duty-bound to investigate the truth about what one believes and what one ultimately adopts as one's religion and way of life. I have access to all of these sources. Pay us a visit some day at my father's house; my father has all of the main Sunni sources at his disposal there. They are leftover mementoes from my grandfather, of course, who did a lot of research. All of these documents and evidences are available and are at your disposal. Needless to say, everything is also available online nowadays. All of these sources can be viewed in reliable websites, so that with a little research, you and I can discover the truth together. On the condition that we are not blinded by our preconceived notions and prejudices.'

Abdul-Hamīd didn't respond. He reduced his speed. The pickup passed a few derelict houses, which Rasūl viewed with curiosity. There was no sign of life in them. He thought of all of the people who lived within these derelict walls who had had a thousand beliefs and aspirations, and who have died and were now buried beneath the earth, and who will be questioned about the veracity of their beliefs as well as their actions in the hereafter.

As he was staring at the derelict houses, he said, 'The Prophet of God said that "the bond or 'cord' which we must hold fast to and not draw apart from is my *wasī* (heir, successor, and legatee) Ali." Two conclusions can be drawn from this hadith report. The first is that Ali is the pillar upon which Islamic unity is to be erected. And the second is that because the Prophet used the word *wasī*, it is clear that he did in fact have an heir, successor, and legatee, and that his heir, successor, and legatee was designated by him.'

Abdul-Hamīd glanced at Rasūl and asked, 'I think you must have studied religion.'

Rasūl shook his head, shrugged, and said, 'No.'

Abdul-Hamīd said, 'I don't believe you! I think your response was insincere.'

Rasūl said, 'I have never studied religion formally in any *hawza* or seminary. But my father and grandfather both had formal religious educations, and I was raised among them and their books and studies and lectures from early childhood.'

Abdul-Hamīd asked, 'What's your father's name?'

Rasūl said, 'Ali'

Abdul-Hamīd nodded and said, 'There. Ali again. Ali everywhere. It seems Ali is everywhere with you Shī'a. What's your grandfather's name?'

Rasūl smiled and said, 'His name is Ali too.'

Abdul-Hamīd looked at Rasūl with surprise and said in a raised voice, '*Both* are named Ali?? Father and son both?!'

'Yes. What's the problem with that? As a matter of fact, Imam Husain was asked why he had named all of his sons Ali. His response was that if God had given him more sons, he would have named all of them Ali too. From the intensity of his love of his father, Imam Ali.'

'Well, at least they named you Rasūl,' Abdul-Hamīd said, keeping his eyes on the road.

'Actually, my name is Ali too, that's what my birth certificate says; it's just that the guys at uni call me Rasūl.'

Abdul-Hamīd's mouth was agape. He shook his head and said, 'Then what they say about how the Shī'a worship Ali is not really too far from the truth, is it?'

Rasūl said, 'Worshipping anyone or anything other than God is *kufr* (unbelief; idolatry). Anyone who worships Imam Ali, or who considers him to be God, is considered by us to be a *kāfir* (unbeliever; idolater), and an apostate (*murtad*). Worship and devotion are the exclusive province of God and of no one and nothing else.'

Abdul-Hamīd said, 'Yes. But the act of prostration (*sajda*) is also the exclusive province of God, yet you extremist Shī'a prostrate yourselves before Imam Ali's shrine and the shrine of your other Imams. You can't deny this, can you? I've seen it on numerous occasions on national television myself.'

This brought a smile to Rasūl's face. He said, 'What you have seen is not an act of prostration in worship before an idol. Sure, it's certainly possible for some of us to prostrate ourselves before the shrines of the Imams because of the great love and devotion that we have for them. People might even rub their foreheads and faces on the soil before their shrines as an act of humility. But these acts do not equate with the Imams being worshipped by them. We Shī'a are monotheists who only worship God; we do not worship the Imams, and never have. Read the *ziārāt*[7] that have been composed by the

---

[7] [*Zīārat*, plural: *zīārāt*: 1. The act of making pilgrimage to a pilgrimage site, usually a shrine of a prophet, imam or *imamzāda* (the progeny of an imam); 2. A liturgical form of supplication or ritual prayer recited specifically during one's pilgrimage to a sacred shrine or location. The Āshūrā *Zīārat* is a leading case in point. This second meaning is what is intended here.]

Infallible Imams: all of them begin with a testimony to the unicity of God, and of His not having any partners whatsoever. The Shī'a believe the Imams to be God's bondsmen, God's chosen bondsmen. Besides, it is not as if anyone can be at all aware of the intention held in the hearts of those who prostrate themselves before the shrines of the Imams. All of these displays of affection, such as these prostration and kissing the thresholds and frames of the portals to the shrines of the Imams, are only out of respect for them and the humility that people feel relative to their exalted spiritual stations, and are merely an indication of their acceptance of their exalted spiritual stations.'

Rasūl paused for a few moments, then continued, as if with an afterthought, 'I hasten to add that a prostration of worship is only performed for God. But there are other kinds of prostrations that do not denote worship, such as the prostration of the angels before Adam, or the prostration of Joseph's brothers before him, both of which appear in the Quran.'

Abdul-Hamīd was taken aback, as if taken by surprise by these arguments. Rasūl continued, 'The same person who commanded the angels to prostrate themselves before Adam also commanded us to the love of and absolute obedience to the Infallible Imams.'

3

The small village of Bīrāh could now be seen in the distance. Abdul-Hamīd pointed to it and said, 'That's Bīrāh.'

Rasūl took the village in. Its dwellings were small and connected to each other. The dome of the mosque was small, as was the hall below it. The roads were narrow. A few people walked up towards the pickup when they saw it approach.

Abdul-Hamīd said, 'Stay close to me. Don't go anywhere without me. You got me?'

Rasūl swallowed and said, 'Yes.'

When the pickup came to a stop, the women stepped down from the back of the truck. Rasūl glanced at Hakīmeh-Khātūn. Seeing her comforted him a little. Abdul-Hamīd opened the door and said to Rasūl, 'Don't speak to anyone. Stick with me wherever I go. Understand?'

'I understand.'

Once Abdul-Hamīd stepped out of the truck, a few men came over and gathered around him. The women who had stepped down from the back of the pickup passed by Abdul-Hamīd. One of them – who seemed to Rasūl to be Rābi'a – thanked Abdul-Hamīd in a loud tone of voice, then turned to Rasūl and gave him a look that was full of enmity. Or maybe it was not enmity; maybe that was just Rasūl's imagination. But whatever it was, it lingered on Rasūl for several moments. Rasūl chose not to look at her directly, preferring to lower his gaze. Rābi'a said something in their local dialect and left. Rasūl didn't know what she said, but whatever it was, it silenced all of the men who had gathered around Abdul-Hamīd, and caused them to stare at Rasūl. Rasūl took a few steps back from the truck. He turned his head, looking to see where Hakīmeh-Khātūn had gone off to, but couldn't find her. She had probably gone into one of the nearby houses. He guessed that she was not able to stay and keep him company among her neighbors and all of those men. And it was the right thing to do; or not to do, as it were. Besides, Hakīmeh-Khātūn was not one to hang out with Rasūl and just talk, even when they were on the university campus. She didn't talk very much, and was bashful and demure. She kept her distance from the menfolk, and she wasn't one to hang out and chat and laugh with other students. And this was the quality that Rasūl saw in Hakīmeh-Khātūn that he was so attracted to.

The day that he saw Hakīmeh-Khātūn for the first time in the library, he asked the librarian, 'Who's the girl who wears that complete *hijāb* (the Muslim dress code of modesty)?'

It took him two months to work up the courage just to have someone hand her a book on his behalf. He had given the book to one of the girls who was in the library and had said, 'Please give this book to that girl. Tell her it's an *amānat* from me (that she should keep it in trust for me).'

The book was a digest of *al-Murāji'āt*.[8] He then gave her the book *Munāżire-ye Husnīye*, followed by the single-volume edition of Allāma Amīnī's *al-Ghadīr*. He continued to do this for a whole year, without getting a single reaction out of her. Not a word, and no written message wither. The books were returned by that same girl who worked in the library, who would say, 'Here you are. She thanked you very kindly.'

Then one day, the girl who was acting as the intermediary got tired of doing so and said, 'Why don't you go and give her the book yourself?'

Rasūl had just stared at her and said, 'I don't know.'

And he really didn't know. Everything proceeded in silence for two years, until the Eid al-Ghadīr festivities of last year which Hakīmeh-Khātūn attended. There, she saw Rasūl standing in a quiet corner and came up to him and returned his copy of *Peshāwar Nights* that he had lent her, and said without looking at him, 'Thank you. I wanted to thank you in person, that's all.'

Hakīmeh-Khātūn left after that, and Rasūl kept repeating her last words to him for a whole week: 'That's all... that's all...'

---

[8] [https://www.al-islam.org/al-murajaat-abd-al-husayn-sharaf-al-din-al-musawi]

There was something in her presence that Rasūl liked. He hadn't seen her face and eyes completely even once. Once he went up to the librarian and asked, 'What books has this girl borrowed from the library?'

He was surprised to see the list of the books she had borrowed. All of them were about the Infallible Imams and about Lady Fātima.

Abdul-Hamīd's voice brought Rasūl back from his thoughts. 'It's time for the noon prayer.'

Rasūl was still looking for Hakīmeh-Khātūn. He nodded to Abdul-Hamīd and said, 'Could you just give me a hand to take my bike down?'

Abdul-Hamīd focused on Rasūl's face. He thought he might have detected a hint of trepidation. He smiled and said, 'You've gone all white. Are you OK?'

'Yeah, I'm fine.'

He avoided looking directly at Abdul-Hamīd so that he would not detect his trepidation. He walked over to the pickup's tailgate. Abdul-Hamīd nodded and said nothing, then climbed up onto the truck's bed and helped Rasūl lower the bike. Rasūl walked the bike a ways and parked it under a tree. Abdul-Hamīd came up to him and looked at him with concern, then opened the button on the sleeve of the hand that had been bandaged. He rolled the sleeve up and examined the bandage. He then nodded his head in approval and said with a smile, 'See, I'm not just a history teacher. I know something of nursing as well.'

He gently placed a hand on Rasūl's shoulder and continued, 'I think of you as my brother, and you are my guest now.'

Rasūl looked at him and a small smile broke out on his face, but he didn't say anything.

Abdul-Hamīd continued, 'I don't say that there are no differences between us. Differences exist. But I have no enmity towards you.'

He turned towards the village and pointed to the dwellings and said, 'There is no one in this village that has any enmity with you. No one!'

Rasūl, who seemed to be a little calmer, nodded and said, 'Thank you.'

They made their ritual ablutions together and headed for the prayer hall to make their prayers. The mosque was very small. It was the size of a single room in a regular house. The sound of the *ażān*, the call to prayer, sounded, and one by one people made their way into the prayer hall. They gave Rasūl a lingering look and then continued on their way to the front of the prayer hall. Rasūl knew that this was how people were in far-away villages: they stared at strangers out of curiosity. Every one of them who stopped to greet Abdul-Hamīd also extended a hand to Rasūl and gave him their *salāms*.

Abdul-Hamīd slowly inclined his head towards Rasūl and asked him, 'Do you want me to go and get you a flat stone for your prostrations?'[9]

Rasūl smiled and asked, 'There isn't a problem with that?'

Abdul-Hamīd said, 'Why should there be a problem? You need to make your prayers in the way that you see fit.'

Taking a small piece of baked clay wrapped in a small piece of green velvet out of his jacket pocket and showing it to Abdul-Hamīd, Rasūl said, 'That's very considerate of you, but it won't be necessary. I always carry one with me.'

'You don't need to participate in our congregation. You can just go in the back and make your prayers there if you prefer.' He pointed to a corner in the back. Rasūl stood up with some hesitance and made his way to the back of the room and stood at the ready to start his prayers. Now everyone's head was turned towards him, and everyone in the mosque was staring at him. After the prayers, Abdul-Hamīd came up to him and said, 'Now let's go to my brother's house.'

He meant Hakīmeh-Khātūn's house. It was a plain and unassuming house made with large old bricks in two stories. They climbed the stairs and sat down in a room, reclining on *poshtīs*, [the firm cushions that are arranged against the walls

---

[9] [In imitation of the exemplary model of the Prophet and the Imams, and based on hadith reports instructing them to this effect, the Shī'a must place their foreheads on earth (or, by extension, baked clay) when making their ritual devotions. In compliance with this sacred instruction, they thus usually place their foreheads on a small cake of baked clay, but a stone will also serve this same purpose.]

which act as recliners]. There was a calligraphic image with the words *Yā Allāh* framed on one of the walls. Hakīmeh-Khātūn's mother entered the room after a few minutes carrying a pitcher of a chilled fruit cordial and some glasses. Abdul-Hamīd introduced her to Rasūl. 'This is Hakīmeh-Khātūn's mother.'

Rasūl rose in a sign of respect. When Hakīmeh-Khātūn's mother sat down, Abdul-Hamīd talked a little about Rasūl and the reason for his visit. Hakīmeh-Khātūn's mother sat at an angle such that her face would not be visible to Rasūl. There was a black cloth covering that covered all of her face other than her eyes, which were angled towards Abdul-Hamīd. Hakīmeh-Khātūn's mother sat and listened in attentive silence to all of Abdul-Hamīd's words.

When he had finished his explanations, she slowly turned her head towards Rasūl, looked at him and said, 'Whatever Allāh wants will occur. My desire is the same as that of Hakīmeh-Khātūn's. The only thing I want from you is for you to respect our *madhhab* – [the creedal basis and juridical rite that they follow]. That is all I ask.'

Having said her peace, she stood up and left the room accompanied by Abdul-Hamīd, not even waiting for Rasūl to respond to what she had said, and leaving him alone in the room. Earlier, Rasūl had thought that Hakīmeh-Khātūn would probably come into the room with her mother. He wanted to see her again, even if only for a few minutes. There was something in her glances that calmed him down. It was something like a light which Rasūl really, really liked. Abdul-Hamīd said a *yā allāh* and entered the room after an appropriate pause, moving aside the white veil that acted to partition the room.[10]

He gave Rasūl a big smile and said, 'Lunch is ready.'

He looked at the small window of the room. 'I can open this window if it's too warm.' Not waiting for an answer, he went over to the window and opened it. He glanced out at the street, then went back towards Rasūl and sat next to him and said, 'After lunch, we will be joined by two other people.'

Rasūl asked with surprise, 'Two other people?'

Abdul-Hamīd nodded in affirmation and said, 'Yes. Hakīmeh-Khātūn's uncle has come over from Bandar Abbās to see you. His name is Abdullāh.'

Rasūl asked, 'He knows about this?'

Abdul-Hamīd asked, 'Shouldn't he be informed? A suitor has come for his niece, and a Shī'a suitor at that.'

Rasūl said nothing. Abdul-Hamīd continued, 'The *imām-e jamā'at* (prayer leader) of the mosque will also be coming. We call him Sheikh Mālik. Remember that Hakīmeh-Khātūn's mother and all of the people of Bīrāh give great credence to what Sheikh Mālik has to say.'

Rasūl gave a bitter smile and said, 'I thought I only had to speak with Hakīmeh-Khātūn's family.'

Abdul-Hamīd became somewhat indignant and said, 'That is all that it is. I'm her *amū* (paternal uncle), and Abdullāh is her *dāī* (maternal uncle).'

---

[10] [This is a habit that Muslims have when entering a room. It is done in case there is a female present who is not properly veiled, and it gives them notice either to veil themselves or to ask for time to do so before the *nāmahram* male can enter the room.]

'But what about Sheikh Mālik?'

Abdul-Hamīd said, 'Sheikh Mālik is different. He is present in all *khāstegārīs* – whenever a suitor comes to ask for someone's hand in marriage. You can't expect him not to be present in this one, where the suitor is Shī'a, no less. He has to see you, sooner or later...'

Then, as if he remembered something, he touched his forehead with the palm of his hand and said, 'What am I saying? Sheikh Mālik can't "see" you!'

'Can't see me?'

Abdul-Hamīd nodded and said, 'Yes, he's blind. He was blinded in one of the terrorist operations of Abdul-Mālik Rīgī. He had gone to see his daughter Āisha in Zāhedān. Abdul-Mālik Rīgī's thugs blew up the minibus that he was in. Everyone lost their life except for three people, one of whom was Sheikh Mālik, who was blinded.'

A few minutes later, the table-spread was laid out on the floor for lunch. No one joined their company for lunch, and it was just Abdul-Hamīd and Rasūl who sat on the floor with the table-spread between them to have lunch. The food was a kind of stew. Rasūl liked how it tasted, even though he had never seen such a dish before and didn't even know its name. Something told him that Hakīmeh-Khātūn had made it.

While they were having their meal, Abdul-Hamīd asked, 'What does your father do for a living?'

Rasūl said, 'He is a bricklayer.'

Abdul-Hamīd said with surprise, 'Huh! I thought he was a cleric.'

Rasūl responded, 'Yes, you're right. But he lays bricks to make ends meet.'

When the table-spread was cleared, they sat back and relaxed for a few minutes. A relatively cool breeze made its way into the room. Abdul-Hamīd said, 'Let me tell you something about Sheikh Mālik – but you didn't hear it from me. Our beliefs and his are not the same. Sheikh Mālik is edging towards another direction. He's heading down a path which cannot end well. I wanted you to know that what Sheikh Mālik says does not necessarily represent my views or the views of Hakīmeh-Khātūn's family. Even Aghā Abdullāh doesn't think the way Sheikh Mālik does. Sheikh Mālik's views are closer to that of the Saudi's or the extremists in Pakistan. If I hear a well-reasoned argument, I will submit to it; I will kneel before it and accept it. And if I realize that I have been mistaken, I will admit my mistake. Or at least I will stay silent rather than speak up for what is wrong. So if you see Sheikh Mālik come and sit here, it is because of the influence that he has in Bīrāh. I have never heard him curse Abdul-Mālik Rīgī, even though he himself was blinded by him!'

They talked in this vein for a few more minutes, after which they heard someone saying *yā allāh, yā allāh* from the other side of the white curtained partition. Then the veil was slowly pulled aside and Hakīmeh-Khātūn's uncle Abdullāh entered the room. Rasūl stood up and shook his hand. Abdullāh was a portly, dark-complected man. The creases in his face were an indication of the fact that he was a man with extensive life-experience. His hair was cropped short, as if he had recently shaved his head. The buttons of his white shirt were open down to his chest, exposing a nest of curly hair. He had a thick mustache that covered his upper lip. He sat opposite Rasūl and placed the cigarette he was holding in his mouth. He leaned back on a *poshtī* and made small-talk with Abdul-Hamīd for a few minutes.

Rasūl's head was lowered and he was looking at the colors of the flowers in the faded carpet he was sitting on. The flowers were in a design that included a small bird that was positioned on a branche of a tree; a pattern that repeated itself throughout the carpet. Rasūl understood from what they were talking about that Abdullāh was a truck driver who trucked cargo from Shīrāz and Kermān to Bandar-Abbās.

Abdullāh turned towards Rasūl and asked him through a fog of white cigarette smoke, 'How long have you known Hakīmeh-Khātūn?'

Rasūl paused for a moment and calmly said, 'Two years, or a little longer.'

Abdullāh took a drag from his cigarette. Although it had only been a couple of hours since Rasūl had gotten to know Abdul-Hamīd, he still wanted him to be his interlocutor as a suitor, and for that not to be anyone else. He felt that it would be more difficult to establish a relationship with Abdullāh.

Abdullāh nodded and stared into Rasūl's eyes and asked, 'How much have you talked with each other? How many times?'

Abdullāh's look was cold and very serious.

Rasūl said, 'Very little, and very briefly.'

Abdullāh asked again without a pause, 'How many times?'

Rasūl shrugged, 'I don't remember how many times. But the conversations were never extended or long. We've talked about university and our classes; that kind of thing.'

'Only about university and your classes?'

'Yes.'

4

Rasūl thought to himself that he hadn't appreciated the value of talking with Abdul-Hamīd and that he had been ungrateful, and that now, God had sent Abdullāh to confront him instead. He knew only too well that his father would not have been willing to sit in such a gathering even for a minute. He raised his head and noticed that Abdullāh was staring at him intently; staring into his eyes now. It seemed as if he was not convinced by Rasūl's answer. But Rasūl had spoken the truth, and the two of them had not really talked that much. It was not like they hadn't talked at all; they had. But Rasūl was not one to hang out and talk for hours, flirting with each other as other girls and boys do. The two of them had talked a few times, and briefly at that.

On the last couple of occasions, they had sat on the grass in front of the university's main building and had talked about marriage and the *khāstegārī* or marriage proposal rite,

and the intensity of their attraction to each other's personality;
but they had kept even this conversation brief, and had done
so at a distance, observing all of the requirements of proper
Islamic etiquette. Throughout all of this, Hakīmeh-Khātūn kept
her head down, participating in the discussions with a modesty
that was her own style, shying away from Rasūl's amorous
glances.

Abdullāh extinguished the butt of his cigarette in an
ashtray, blew out a large plume of white smoke, and asked
with a certain cunning, 'If all you talked about was the
university and classes, then how did you propose to her?'

Rasūl expected such a question. He looked at Abdul-
Hamīd and Abdullāh and said, 'That was just a few sentences.
A few short sentences.'

Abdullāh nodded and said nothing. Then they heard
someone saying *yā allāh, yā allāh* again from the other side of
the white curtain, which was then pushed aside, after which
Sheikh Mālik entered the room together with a youth who was
holding his hand and who acted as his guide. All three men
stood up in a gesture of respect for the new arrival. Sheikh
Mālik was short. He was wearing a white *shalwār khamīz* set,
as was the traditional custom in those parts. The pair of
trousers of the set were very short, so much so that his dark
skinny shins could be seen. He was holding a long walking
stick, and his white beard came down to the bottom of his
chest. He wore a white *kufi* or skullcap which was perhaps an
indication of a certain degree of education in a *madrasa* or
Islamic seminary. Sheikh Mālik's guide took him over to the
wall and guided him down, then looked at Rasūl, who nodded

and said '*Salām.*' The youth passed by him on his way out without acknowledging Rasūl's greeting. He said goodbye to Abdul-Hamīd and Abdullāh and left.

Sheikh Mālik sat down and let out a loud sigh. He placed his hand on his knees and said, 'Those stairs will be the end of me.'

He then said something in their local dialect which seemed to be about the difficulty of the stairs. Abdul-Hamīd and Abdullāh nodded and smiled. Abdul-Hamīd said, 'It's good of you to come. You are very welcome.'

Sheikh Mālik nodded and said, 'If we are to start the meeting, we should do so by reciting some verses of the Quran.'

Abdul-Hamīd rose and left the room to return shortly with a Quran. He sat down, opened the Quran, and started reading some of its verses. He recited a few of the short *sūras* (partitions or "chapters") from the back of the book melodically. Sheikh Mālik nodded with approval at the end of each *sūra,* saying *allāh, allāh* as an indication of his appreciation of the recital. It was clear to see that the recital of the *sūras* put him in a different state of mind.

When the recital was over, Abdul-Hamīd closed the Quran, kissed it, and placed it reverently beside the wall. The room became quiet. Sheikh Mālik cleared his throat quietly and said, '*B'ism'illāh ar-rahmān ar-rahīm.* I will start with a short question from this young Shī'a man who is your guest.'

Rasūl was staring at Sheikh Mālik's unseeing eyes.

Sheikh Mālik continued, 'I would like to know why he has come here to propose to a Sunni girl, rather than going to propose to a Shī'a girl.'

Abdul-Hamīd and Abdullāh both turned their heads towards Rasūl. Rasūl looked at the sheikh's black cane and said, 'Maybe it was my destiny to come here. I think of Hakīmeh-Khātūn as a true Muslim. For me, Hakīmeh-Khātūn is no different than a Shī'a girl. As a matter of fact, she has certain merits of character that I have not seen in other Shī'a girls.'

Abdul-Hamīd seemed to like this answer. He nodded in agreement, and as a point of pride. And even though Abdullāh was still playing hard to get, he nodded in approval too.

Sheikh Mālik said, 'But for me, you *are* different than all of the Sunni boys, and will never be the same as them. Do you know why I say this? Because I cannot tell a lie, as I believe that liars are enemies of God, and that the Prophet's *sunna* – his exemplary model or paradigmatic example; his mode of conduct – consists of sincerity and truthfulness.'

Rasūl said nothing. Hearing this kind of talk, he knew that things would not proceed as he had hoped they would. Perhaps Hakīmeh-Khātūn should have somehow prevented Sheikh Mālik's presence in the meeting. Or perhaps there was nothing she could do, and the matter was out of her hands. He knew that if this meeting did not end well, he would probably have to keep his distance from Hakīmeh-Khātūn forever. On the way over, when he got on his motorcycle and headed over to Bīrāh from Serāt, he thought that he would be speaking to

Abdul-Hamīd and Hakīmeh-Khātūn's mother. But now Sheikh Mālik and Abdullāh had appeared on the scene, and had erected a high wall between him and his aspirations. Rasūl thought that he would probably be asked about his future profession, his source of income, and about his family. And about why he loved Hakīmeh-Khātūn, and how it was that he came to Bīrāh to propose to a Sunni girl when there were so many Shī'a girls available closer at hand in the university and among his friends and extended relatives. He raised his head and looked at Sheikh Mālik, whose eyes were open. There was no obvious sign of blindness in his eyes, such that if one did not know he was blind, one might not have been able to surmise that he was.

Sheikh Mālik continued, 'If we were talking about the sale of a property or a car or something, I would not feel obliged to involve myself, but what is at stake here is the fate of a young lady. A young lady who shares our beliefs and is Sunni, concerning whom I have certain obligations and responsibilities, and about whom I will be held to account on the Day of Judgment by God and by His prophet, to whom I will ultimately be held to account. The truth is that I do not have any good recollections about these kinds [mixed] of marriages. In this same Sīstān province, a wealthy Shī'a boy came and proposed to a Sunni girl. His name was Mahdi. I knew the girl well. And I knew and know both her parents well also. They are a renowned family in Sīstān. This Shī'a boy came and married this Sunni girl. After six months, they started quarreling, and they ended up getting divorced. Do you know why? Because that Shī'a boy would not stop his cursing and imprecations of the Prophet's august *sahāba* (companions).'

Sheikh Mālik raised his hands. 'I have come here only to tell this young Shī'a this one sentence, and then take my leave.'

Abdul-Hamīd and Abdullāh focused on the sheikh, who said, 'Even if the sky should fall down to the Earth, Sunnis will still be Sunnis, and Shī'a will still be Shī'a. Nothing can change this. The truth is just what I say: our beliefs and yours are not the same. If we use God, the Quran, the Prophet, and the *qibla* (the direction of prayer), that is all well and good, and many of our differences will be resolved with these commonalities. But the problem is that the Shī'a are not satisfied with these things that we hold in common. They accept God, the Quran, and the Prophet, but they want to add a whole bunch of other things to God's religion. And then they insist with all insolence that the things that they have added to the religion are an integral part of it. What raises my ire so much is that they do not stop short even of that, and go on to insist that God's religion is not and cannot be complete without these admixtures!'

He raised his head, paused for a short while, and then said, 'Now if your guest is one of these extremist (*gālī*) Shī'a, I am not at all optimistic about the prospects of this union.'

Abdul-Hamīd nodded and said, 'Your points are very well taken, but I would like to put something to you.'

Sheikh Mālik extended his skinny legs and let out a moan and said, 'I'm listening.'

Abdul-Hamīd said, 'I have talked with this young man from the time it took us to drive from the fork in the road that leads to Bīrāh. There are two points that occur to me that I thought it would be helpful to mention to you. The fact that this young man has come all this way and has chosen to propose to a girl from Bīrāh is in itself a good sign. After all, he knew that he would be proposing to a Suni family. He has stepped forward with certain knowledge, and this stepping forward in itself has a welcome signification in that it means that he has no enmity with us, and his heart is pure of such emotions and ideas.'

Abdullāh who was listening closely nodded his head in approval.

Abdul-Hamīd continued, 'Let me be frank and say it straight: according to what I have been able to understand, this young man is not an extremist Shī'a, or as you put it a "*gālī*" Shī'a; those who do nothing but curse the *sahāba*. We have had a discussion with one another. As a matter of fact, this young man believes in Islamic unity.'

Sheikh Mālik said, 'How do you know that what he believes is that which he has told you?!' Maybe he is dissimulating (*taqīya*) and hiding his true beliefs!'

Abdul-Hamīd glanced at Rasūl and said nothing.

Sheikh Mālik said, 'Give him that Quran so that I can put an end to all this.'

Abdul-Hamīd looked at Abdullāh and Rasūl. He was wondering what he should do. He reached for the Quran and gave it to Rasūl.

Sheikh Mālik said, 'Place you hand on the Quran, young man!'

Rasūl placed his hand on the Quran with some reluctance.

Sheikh Mālik said, 'Now that you have your hand on the Quran, swear that you do not believe in the cursing and imprecation of the Companions of the Prophet. May God's curse be upon you if you lie. Remember that your hand is on the Quran.'

Abdullāh and Abdul-Hamīd stared intently at Rasūl's eyes.

With his hand still on the Quran, Rasūl said, 'I swear on this sacred book that I have never cursed the faithful and august companions of the Prophet of God, and that I do not believe in doing so.'

Abdul-Hamīd smiled when he heard Rasūl say these words, and Abdullāh nodded in approval.

Sheikh Mālik said, 'While you still have your hand on the Quran, state what your opinion is about the Mother of the Faithful, Lady Āisha.'

Rasūl said, 'I follow the Prophet of God. May God curse anyone who insults the faithful wives of the Prophet of God. My opinion about Lady Āisha is the same as that of the Prophet of God's.'

Sheikh Mālik was silenced. When Abdul-Hamīd saw that the sheikh had become silent, he reached out and took the Quran from Rasūl, and then placed a hand on his shoulder as a sign of his amity. Rasūl smiled and shook his head a little. Sheikh Mālik, who didn't expect Rasūl to place his hand on the

Quran, said, 'In any event, I am not aware of a single issue that these Shī'a have not taken a divisive position on. An example is this business with Ghadīr.'

Abdullāh, who had been reticent up to this point, said, 'Sheikh Mālik, I don't mean to be rude, but we are gathered here to talk about this young man's proposal to Hakīmeh-Khātūn. Ghadīr and these kinds of things have nothing to do with the matter at hand. The fact that this young man has sworn to your questions with his hand on the Quran suffices us. The truth is that I need to go back to Shīrāz by nightfall. Time is short and there is much to discuss. If you don't mind, let us go to the main issue at hand.'

Abdul-Hamīd quickly added, 'Yes, I agree with that.'

Sheikh Mālik said, 'The "main issue at hand" is the fact that you have not properly understood the Shī'a! And until you *do*, you *cannot* give the hand of your girls to them in marriage!!'

The sheikh raised the cuff of his trousers, scratched his knee, and continued, 'Their *skill* lies in their dissimulation.'

Rasūl looked at Abdullāh and Abdul-Hamīd and said, 'Bring the Quran so that I can place my hand on it and swear that like you, we believe that lying is a sin, and believe that the *sunna* of the Prophet of God is nothing but truth-telling and sincerity.'

Sheikh Mālik said, 'I have my doubts about your swearing such oaths! How am I to know that he is telling the truth and is not lying [even then]?!'

For a moment, Rasūl's thoughts went to Hakīmeh-Khātūn. He wondered where she was right now and what she was doing. She was probably sitting somewhere listening to these words. He knew that Hakīmeh-Khātūn would also be distraught at hearing such words being spoken.

Abdul-Hamīd didn't want their voices to be raised such that the neighbors could hear what they were saying, despite the fact that Bīrāh was such a small village that everyone already knew that Hakīmeh-Khātūn had a Shī'a suitor.

Abdul-Hamīd smiled and said, 'It is not as if we have already decided to give the hand of Hakīmeh-Khātūn to this young man. This is just a meeting for us to get to know each other better...'

Abdul-Hamīd's main concern was to calm Sheikh Mālik down so that the neighbors would not hear what was being said. The sheikh's getting angry in their house and under these circumstances did not bode well for their family at all.

Sheikh Mālik said, 'I'm not talking specifically about this young man who is your guest. I'm talking about tomorrow and the future. If you see this young man sitting here all quiet without saying anything, it is because now it is we who have the upper hand. It is because we hold the reins in our hands now; *we* are the deciders. What is important is how this young man will act when the bargain has been struck and he is in change. Have you given any thought to that day and eventuality?'

Abdul-Hamīd and Abdullāh just looked at each other.

Sheikh Mālik continued, 'Let us assume that this young man is righteous, pious, and morally upstanding. But

what about his family? What about his father and mother? His
brothers? His aunts and uncles? Indeed, why are his parents
not present here today? Do they have the same beliefs as this
young man, or are they Shī'a of the extremist bent?'

Rasūl said nothing. The room became silent. Sheikh
Mālik groped for his wooden cane, grabbed it, pointed it at
Rasūl and said, 'Why are you silent? Well?? Say something!
Defend yourself!!'

Rasūl looked at those present in dismay. He gave a
bitter smile and said, 'As God is my witness, if I knew that my
coming here was going to upset you, I would not have come. I
came in order to draw closer to you, not in order to draw
farther apart. And it was with the permission of this family
that I took this step. Hakīmeh-Khātūn herself told me in the
university that Master Abdul-Hamīd has sent a message that
he wanted to see her suitor. Which is why I obeyed and came
here to be at your service. And I have only come to propose a
union, not in order to cause differences between us, or to
cloudy our relations or cause ill feelings. I'm not here to fan
the flames of Sunni/ Shī'a rivalries. Imam Sādiq, unto whom be
God's peace, has commanded us live in amity and peace with
our Sunni brethren, and this is the basis of what we refer to as
Islamic unity.'

Rasūl turned to Sheikh Mālik and continued, 'Sheikh
Mālik, I agree with you. The Sunni and the Shī'a have had
credal differences with each other since the very beginning,
and continue to do so. But these two sects have been living
with each other in this country for centuries. You have your
creed and we have ours. But Islamic unity cannot be attained

with these kinds of aggressive words that make things more rather than less opaque, and with the stoking up of our emotions based on our creedal differences. We must put aside our differences and enmities, and sit down in the company of the Quran, and the words of the Prophet and [the purified and inerrant members of] his Family (*itra*)! True unity can only be reached through logic and reasoned arguments and proofs. I place my hand on the Quran and swear upon the Quran and my honor that I am against the unjust cursing and insulting of anyone.'

Sheikh Mālik laughed at Rasūl, saying, 'You are the first Shīʻa who says you are against cursing and imprecation.'

Rasūl replied, 'Now that things have taken such a turn and you refuse to change your position, will you allow me to put a question to you? It might help us to reach a conclusion faster.'

Sheikh Mālik said very firmly and confidently, 'Ask away. Ask a hundred questions.'

The sheikh's cane was still in his hand and moved in the air whenever he spoke.

Rasūl said, 'If God curses someone, would you also curse that person, or would you still be against cursing and imprecation?'

Sheikh Mālik stayed silent. He didn't say anything. Abdul-Hamīd and Abdullāh looked at him.

Rasūl continued, 'Now what about if the Prophet of God cursed someone? What then? Would you be willing to curse someone whom the Prophet of God himself has cursed?

Or do you not follow the Prophet's exemplary model or mode of conduct (*sīra*) in this case?'

Sheikh Mālik reluctantly said, 'This is not a subject that can be answered with a few sentences. It must be considered in detail first.'

Rasūl looked at Abdullāh and Abdul-Hamīd, and facing Abdullāh, asked, 'Let me ask you. If one of the companions of the Prophet attacked him and injured him by kicking him hard, such that he fell to the ground, would you have any respect or show any deference to such a person?'

Abdullāh said, 'No, never.'

Rasūl smiled and said, 'Then there is no difference between the two of us on this point. Both of us respect and honor those Companions who themselves respect and honor the Prophet of God. In other words, we have not had, nor do we have, any personal animosity or hostility towards any of the Companions as such.'

Abdullāh nodded and said, 'True.'

5

Someone could be heard from behind the curtain saying *yā allāh.*

Rasūl recognized the voice and his heart quivered. How he loved this voice. Abdul-Hamīd stood up and held the curtain to the side with his forearm. Rasūl could see Hakīmeh-Khātūn's narrow fingers. She handed the tray of tea to Abdul-Hamīd, who took it from her, after which Hakīmeh-Khātūn left. Abdullāh lit another cigarette while Abdul-Hamīd was placing the tea glasses in front of his guests. Sheikh Mālik extended his arm, groping to find his glass of tea which he knew had been placed in front of his folded legs. Abdul-Hamīd took two dates from the bowl that was in front of his other guests and gave them to Sheikh Mālik.

Sheikh Mālik took a bite out of one of them and said, 'You are a good young man! But you are immature and inexperienced in the ways of the world. We and your people live together, eat from the same plate, drink from the same cup, sleep in the same beds, and occasionally intermarry; but when it comes to our creedal beliefs, we are separate and far apart. Remember, young man, it was you Shī'a who started this conflict. I'm not talking about today and yesterday. You sowed the seeds of division among the Muslims from the time of the Sermon of Ghadīr Khumm. You gave the lie to the Apostle of God, saying he had designated Ali as his successor, whereas God knows that is not the case and never was.'

Rasūl reached towards his glass of tea. It was still very hot. He shook his head, looked at Sheikh Mālik, and said, 'We don't make any such claim.'

Abdul-Hamīd and Abdullāh looked at Rasūl with surprise. Abdullāh exhaled a large plume of white smoke, and stared at Rasūl. Sheikh Mālik tried to cleared the air of the cigarette smoke with his hand, and said, 'Really? Here! *Another* lie! Do you not claim that the Prophet of God raised Ali's hand in Ghadīr Khumm and designated him as his successor?'

Rasūl said patiently, 'The *Prophet* did not do that.'

Sheikh Mālik asked with greater consternation, 'The Prophet did not *do* that?? Then who *did*?'

Rasūl said, 'It was God's will. *God* chose Imam Ali to be the successor of the Prophet.'

Abdul-Hamīd and Abdullāh looked at each other with surprise. Abdullāh chewed the filter of his cigarette, then exhaled some more smoke.

Rasūl said, 'The Prophet raised Ali's hand at the express order he received from God. This act was so important that if he had not done it, it would be as if the entirety of his mission and ministry was incomplete.' Rasūl then quoted the following verse from the Quran.

$$\text{يَا أَيُّهَا الرَّسُولُ بَلِّغْ مَا أُنزِلَ إِلَيْكَ مِن رَّبِّكَ ۖ وَإِن لَّمْ تَفْعَلْ فَمَا بَلَّغْتَ رِسَالَتَهُ ۚ وَاللَّهُ يَعْصِمُكَ مِنَ النَّاسِ ۗ إِنَّ اللَّهَ لَا يَهْدِي الْقَوْمَ الْكَافِرِينَ ﴿٦٧﴾}$$

[5:67] O apostle! Announce all that has been sent down [to you] from on high by thy Lord of Providence (*rabb*): for unless thou doest it fully, [it would be as if] thou wilt not have delivered His message [at all]. And God will protect thee from [the mischief of unbelieving] men: behold, God does not guide people who refuse to acknowledge the truth.

Rasūl then paused for effect, then asked, 'Do you know what this means? It means that you can put all of the twenty-three years of the ministry of the Prophet on one pan of the scales, and his announcing God's choice of Ali as his successor in the other pan!'

Sheikh Mālik raised his glass of tea to his lips and drank some tea. Rasūl was surprised at how the sheikh was able to drink the tea while it was still so hot. Sheikh Mālik returned the glass of tea to its saucer, and then started straightening and rubbing his legs, as if he was trying to work out a cramp.

Rasūl smiled and said, 'I have not come here to talk about our differences. But I do think that anyone who denies the truth and significance of the Sermon of Ghadīr Khumm casts a doubt on God's justice.'

Sheikh Mālik turned his head towards Abdul-Hamīd and Abdullāh, and said, 'For the Shī'a, Ali is the criterion for everything. The criterion for one's monotheism is Ali! The criterion for one's religion and faith are Ali! The criterion for being a Muslim is Ali! Ali and the Sermon of Ghadīr Khumm, and nothing else!'

Rasūl turned to Abdul-Hamīd, who was looking at him in silence. Sheikh Mālik raised his voice in anger, and shaking his cane in the air, said, 'How *dare* you spew this nonsense! What in *hell* does Ghadīr have to do with God's justice?!'

Sheikh Mālik's voice had now been raised to such a pitch that it scared Abdul-Hamīd. Sheikh Mālik's face had turned purple, and his jugular vein had become very pronounced. Abdul-Hamīd got up and closed the window so as not to let the noise out. He looked at the sky. It seemed to Rasūl that he had seen something in the sky that had attracted his attention. He came back and sat next to Sheikh Mālik.

In order to calm Sheikh Mālik down and take control of the direction of the conversation, he turned to Rasūl and said, 'What evidence do you have when you say that anyone who denies the truth and significance of the Sermon of Ghadīr Khumm casts a doubt on God's justice.'

Rasūl shook his head in dismay and said, 'Let us leave the discussion there and not pursue it any further.'

Abdul-Hamīd said, 'No! Tell me! I want to hear what you have to say.'

Rasūl said, 'Do you believe that God is just?'

Abdul-Hamīd replied, 'What kind of question is that? Of *course* I think God is just!'

Rasūl said, 'How did God guide the nations of the past?'

Abdul-Hamīd said, 'He sent prophets to them to guide them.'

Rasūl nodded his affirmation and asked, 'Who has God sent for your and my guidance? Why is it that those of us who live in these times do not have a guide sent by God?'

Abdul-Hamīd said nothing. He was mulling over Rasūl's question in his mind, trying to find an answer. It was a strange question that had never occurred to him.

Rasūl continued, 'God sent the prophet Jesus to the Christians, and the prophet Moses to the Jews. He sent David, Solomon, Noah, and Abraham, and the prophet Sālih to other peoples and places. The real question is, Who is the guide for those who lived and continue to live after the time of the prophet Muhammad? Has God abandoned us without a guide?'

When Abdul-Hamīd said nothing, Rasūl continued, 'Would that not be prejudicial and contrary to the principle of God's justice? Would one then not be able to raise an objection on the Day of Judgment, saying, "Do not expect me, O Lord, to be one of your guided servants, as You did not send me a divine guide!"?'

Sheikh Mālik spoke up with the same anger that he had displayed earlier. 'You accuse God of favoritism and being unjust?! God has not stopped His guidance of us. Before the Apostle of God, guidance was the responsibility of prophets and apostles, and after Muhammad, the responsibility for guidance rests with the Quran!!'

Abdul-Hamīd and Abdullāh both nodded in response to this assertion, content that Sheikh Mālik was able to respond to Rasūl's question and save them from the bind that they were in.

Rasūl looked at Sheikh Mālik and said, 'But the Quran is not sufficient for the guidance of the people.'

Sheikh Mālik said, 'How is it not sufficient?! The Quran is the most complete sacred scripture in the whole world!'

Rasūl said, 'If the Quran is the most complete sacred scripture in the whole world, tell me where in the Quran it is stated that the morning prayers consist of two cycles?'

Sheikh Mālik didn't have anything to say to that. He knew that there was no revelation in the Quran about the number of cycles of the morning prayers. Abdul-Hamīd and Abdullāh looked expectantly to Sheikh Mālik for an answer, but Sheikh Mālik remained quiet.

Rasūl continued, 'We pray the morning prayer in two cycles because the Prophet of God commanded us to do so. Thus, not all of the requirements of our religion appear in the Quran; or if they are, we are not able to discover them or understand them. God's religion can only be taught to people by God's *hujja*.[11] And you now say that God does not have a

---

[11] [Professor Hāmid Algar provides the following definition: The designation *hujjat* ("proof") given to the Imams has a twofold sense. First, through the qualities they manifest, they are proofs of the existence of God and of the veracity of the religion He has revealed, [and serve the function of acting as

hujja or Imam or guide after the passing of the Prophet?! The Quran will indeed act to guide, but it will only guide the *muttaqīn*, those with *taqwā*[12] – in other words, those who believe in the successors to the Prophet, who are the Twelve Imams.'

Sheikh Mālik shook his head and said, 'This is another one of the claims of the Shī'a who say that the Quran does not guide everyone.'

Rasūl said, 'No. Actually, it is God's word, which appears right in the beginning of Suraᵗ al-Baqara.' Rasūl then quoted the Quranic verse.

ذَلِكَ الْكِتَابُ لَا رَيْبَ ۛ فِيهِ ۛ هُدًى لِّلْمُتَّقِينَ ﴿٢﴾

[2:2] This Divine Writ (*al-kitāb*) – let there be no doubt about it; it is [meant to be] a guidance for all who are weary [of the consequences of one's wrongful actions before God] (*al-muttaqīn*).

---

exemplary models of divinely-sanctioned ethical conduct to be emulated - BAW]. Second, [by serving this function and providing such an example,] they constitute proofs to be advanced on the Day of Judgment against those who claim they were uninformed of God's law [and moral dispensation].]
[12] [*Taqwā*: a righteousness and pious devotion of the soul and of one's character which is informed by a fear of the potentially everlasting consequences of appearing before God on the Day of Judgement and the prospect of the failure to perform well before one's Lord of Providence and Cherisher (*rabb*) in this ultimate, fateful Judgement.]

Sheikh Mālik said nothing, and Rasūl continued, 'In other words, it is not the case that it is possible for one simply to open the Quran and then somehow be guided! Guidance is in the hands of God Himself, which is realized through His commissioned *hujja*. If it were the case that guidance to God's Way was to be realized through a book, then what would have been the necessity of His commissioning all of the past prophets to their missions?! He could have just sent a book like the Quran to the various peoples prior to the advent of the Quran.'

Rasūl paused to take a sip of his tea, then continued, 'If your claim is true and the Quran can indeed guide all peoples, then surely it would guide everyone to a single Way. So then tell me, why are you Sunni brothers of mine divided into four groups?[13]

The room was silent.

Rasūl continued, 'Or we can look at it from another perspective. Why did God's Apostle not raise the Quran in the air at Ghadīr Khumm? Why did he raise Ali's hand?'

Again, silence.

Rasūl continued, 'Ali's hand was raised because Ali's hand *is* the Quran's hand! Ali's hand is the hand of divinely-

---

[13] The reference here is to the four religio-juridical Sunni rites: The Hanafis, who follow Abū-Hanīfa, the Mālikis who follow Mālik ibn Anas, the Shāfi'is, who follow Muhammad ibn Idrīs ash-Shāfi'ī, and the Hanbalis, who follow Ahmad ibn al-Hanbal. These four sects are not agreed in terms of the ordinances of the law, in terms of the principles of jurisprudence, or in terms of their creedal beliefs [in which there are other major divisions]. Prior to their consolidation, there were ten such sects, whose numbers were reduced to four in the fourth Islamic century.

inspired guidance! If one binds Ali's hands with rope, it is as if he has bound the hands of God's guidance with rope. This is the meaning of the words of the Prophet of God who said, "Ali is [always] with *al-haqq*[14] and *al-haqq* is [always] with Ali".[15]

Sheikh Mālik said, '"God's hand"? Is that not a form of idolatry?!'

Rasūl replied, 'This is an expression that the second caliph used in referring to Imam Ali. During one of the Hajj pilgrimages one year, a youth was molesting a woman. Ali saw what was taking place and struck a blow at him in order to prevent him from continuing to molest the poor woman. The insolent youth went to the second caliph, complaining that Ali had beaten him out of the House of God. The second caliph said, "God's eye saw you, and God's hand beat you".'[16]

Sheikh Mālik didn't say anything more to this. It was obvious that he was not doing too well, and that he was not too pleased with Rasūl's verbosity. Suddenly a loud noise was heard from outside the house. Rasūl and Abdul-Hamīd and Abdullāh looked at each other in surprise. Abdullāh got up and

---

[14] [*Al-Haqq* is a key Quranic term whose meaning has three main facets or components: reality, truth, and justice, all of which are contained in a single word because the three concepts are inextricably interconnected in the Quranic worldview. I have left the word untranslated here because in this context, all three facets apply. *Al-Haqq* is also one of the Names of God.]

[15] This hadith report is narrated by Āisha as reported by Tirmidhī in his *Sahīh*, 2:289, and in *Qāyat al-Marām*, 5:283. [See also Ibn Qutaybah, *al-Imāmah wa al-Siyāsah*, Vol. I, p. 68; Ibrāhim b. Muhammad al-Juwayni, *Farā'id as-Simtayn*, Chapter 37; al-Khatīb al-Baghdādi, *at-Tārīkh al-Baghdād*, Vol. IV, p. 21; Fakhr ad-Dīn ar-Rāzī, *al-Fusul al-Muhimmah*.]

[16] This hadith report also appears in several Sunni sources.

went to the wooden-framed window, opened it, and looked outside.

Sheikh Mālik turned to him and asked, 'What was that sound?'

His voice trembled. His face was still purple. Abdullāh looked at the sky, bewildered. He said, 'You won't believe it, but that was the clap of a thunderhead.'

Abdul-Hamīd looked at him in disbelief. 'Thunder, you say??'

He got up and went to the window. He stood next to Abdullāh, and the two of them stared at the rain-cloud covered sky of Bīrāh.

Sheikh Mālik asked, 'You mean it's going to rain here? After all these years?'

Abdul-Hamīd and Abdullāh were still staring at the sky. After a little while, they came over to where Rasūl was sitting and sat back down. Abdullāh leaned back against the wall and said, 'I don't ever remember it raining in Bīrāh.'

Abdul-Hamīd started to gather the empty tea glasses and to place them in the tray. He said, 'It has rained once, but that was close to seventy years ago!'

Rasūl looked at Sheikh Mālik and said, 'Will you allow me to put a question to you?'

'Go right ahead.'

Rasūl said, 'Who do you think is more intelligent and knowledgeable, Abu Bakr or the Prophet of God?'

Sheikh Mālik said, 'I consider the Prophet of God to be more intelligent and knowledgeable.'

Rasūl then asked, 'What about Muʿāwiya or the Prophet of God?'

Sheikh Mālik said, 'Again, I consider the Prophet of God to be more intelligent and knowledgeable.'

Rasūl turned to Abdul-Hamīd and Abdullāh. A loud peal of thunder shook the room. Everyone's head turned towards the window.

'Is it really going to rain??'

Abdul-Hamīd smiled and said, 'If God wants to send us his blessings, he will certainly do so.'

Rasūl turned to Abdul-Hamīd and said, 'But I say that the Prophet of God is not more intelligent and knowledgeable than Abu Bakr or Muʿāwiya.'

Abdul-Hamīd looked at him in surprise and asked, 'Why do you say that??'

Rasūl said, 'Because Abu Bakr and Muʿāwiya were intelligent enough to designate a successor for themselves, and not to abandon the Islamic community to the bewilderment of nescience. But the Apostle of God was not intelligent enough to think about this 'trivial' issue, and failed to designate a successor – according to you.'

Abdul-Hamīd went deep into thought. Abdullāh was looking out the window.

Rasūl said, 'Of course, it is better to put it this way, that Abu Bakr and Muʿāwiya are more intelligent even than God, because according to your belief, God didn't designate anyone to guide the people, and left them without a guide and to their own whims.'

Sheikh Mālik said in a loud and angry voice, 'Now you are taunting us!!'

Rasūl said, 'It is not a taunt, dear sheikh. All of what I have said is merely the truths of history. What you believe is respected and cherished, but it is at variance with the evidence provided by the historical record. Leaf through the pages of the formative period of Islam. You will see that Ali is preeminent in *all* attributes compared to all of the Companions. In other words, history tells us that there is no one who is more preeminent than Ali in a single attribute. Ali is preeminent in *everything*! In knowledge; in piety; in asceticism; in sincerity; in courage and valor – in everything. There was never a *jihād* in which Ali didn't participate and come out victorious, and return having vanquished the enemy.[17] Now go and do your research and see which of the Companions fled the scene of battle like a mountain goat.'[18]

Rasūl continued, 'No revelation was ever revealed to the Prophet without his reciting it to Imam Ali, Ali writing it down, and then having the Prophet explain it and teach its hidden meanings to Ali. According to what the Prophet teaches us, he was the most bravehearted and courageous of men, such that he could kill the enemy with a single blow of his sword. Ali ibn Abī-Tālib was someone whom the second caliph considered to be master (*mawlā*) of every true believer

---

[17] See, for example, Ahmad ibn Hanbal's *Musnad*, 1:99; see also *Ma'jam al-Awsat*, 3:87.

[18] See Suyūtī's *ad-Durr al-Manthūr* in the commentary on verses 154-5 of Sūra^t Āl al-'Imrān for a description of the flight of one of the Rightly Guided caliphs from battle.

(*mu'min*); and it is Ali concerning whom the second caliph has admitted that 'Were it not for the presence of Ali, 'Umar would have perished'. The Prophet of God said in glorifying Ali that he was 'the Sword of God' (*saifallāh*).'

Abdul-Hamīd and Abdullāh were listening to Rasūl's words in complete silence.

Rasūl continued, 'The Prophet of God thought of Ali as the best of all creatures (*khayr al-barīa*; see Quran 98:7). And it is stated in your own books that the Prophet designated Ali as his vizier and successor on numerous occasions. How can you think that God would leave people without a guide, and then expect them to be guided?? Upon my word of honor before God, Ali is that very Divinely-designated Guide who was chosen by God, and whom the Prophet of God introduced at Ghadīr Khumm openly and formally as his successor.'

6

The room fell into a deep silence. Sheikh Mālik's face had lost its color, and he kept opening his mouth to say something, then closing it, then opening it again. But he wasn't able to say anything. Abdul-Hamīd got up and went to the window to see if it had started to rain yet.

Rasūl turned to Sheikh Mālik and continued, 'In your own books, Āisha is reported to have narrated that the Prophet of God said that Ali is with that which is right (*al-haqq*) and that, that which is right is with Ali. So then explain why it is that this same Ali, who is with "that which is right", chose to stay in his house and not go to the mosque to pledge allegiance to Abu Bakr?!'

Sheikh Mālik's head was lowered and he was biting his lip. His hands were shaking visibly. It was clear that he was angry and even outraged.

Rasūl continued. 'Have you read this *āya* of the Quran that commands us to *Pay heed unto God, and pay heed unto the*

Apostle, and unto those from among you who have been entrusted with authority?' He then recited the verse in its original Arabic, as usual.

يَا أَيُّهَا الَّذِينَ آمَنُوا أَطِيعُوا اللَّهَ وَأَطِيعُوا الرَّسُولَ وَأُولِي الْأَمْرِ مِنكُمْ ۖ فَإِن تَنَازَعْتُمْ فِي شَيْءٍ فَرُدُّوهُ إِلَى اللَّهِ وَالرَّسُولِ إِن كُنتُمْ تُؤْمِنُونَ بِاللَّهِ وَالْيَوْمِ الْآخِرِ ۚ ذَٰلِكَ خَيْرٌ وَأَحْسَنُ تَأْوِيلًا ﴿٥٩﴾

[4:59] O you who have attained to faith! Pay heed unto God, and pay heed unto the Apostle and unto those from among you who have been entrusted with authority; and if you are at variance over any matter, refer it unto God and the Apostle, if you [truly] believe in God and the Last Day. This is the best [for you], and best in the end.

Sheikh Mālik did not answer his question.

Rasūl said, 'If only just this once, tell me who *those from among you who have been entrusted with authority* are that God has commanded us in the Quran to obey?!'

He looked alternately to Abdul-Hamīd who was still at the window, and to Abdullāh who was leaning against the wall, then repeated his question: 'Who are *those from among you who have been entrusted with authority?'*

Abdul-Hamīd and Abdullāh had no answer and only looked at him.

Rasūl said, 'Are *those from among you who have been entrusted with authority* the kings who are among us? Would

God have commanded us to obey the kings? Well, Nimrod was a king; Pharaoh was a king; the kings of Persia and Byzantium were kings too!'

He fell silent. Abdullāh asked, 'So then who were they?

Rasūl said, 'The Quran tells us to pray. How we are to pray was taught to us by the Prophet of God. The Quran tells us to fast. How we are to fast was taught to us by the Prophet of God. The Quran tells us to go on the Hajj pilgrimage if we are able. How we are to perform the rites of this pilgrimage was taught to us by the Prophet of God. Now the Quran also tells us to obey *those from among you who have been entrusted with authority*, and who these are has also been taught to us by the Prophet of God. We must refer to the words of the Prophet. Ask yourself who these people are and how important they must be for them to have been referred to in the Quran, where God has commanded us to obey them, referring to them alongside His own name and the name of the Prophet. These are, of course, the Twelve Imams of the Shī'a who the Prophet has referred to in the hadith report known as *al-hadīth al-Jābir*, as well as in the Sermon of Ghadīr Khumm, and on numerous other occasions.

Abdul-Hamīd and Abdullāh nodded slowly and looked at each other, deep in thought. Suddenly, Sheikh Mālik placed his hand on the floor and said, '*Yā Allāh*. This is no longer a place for me!'

He placed his cane down on the floor and said, 'We have surrendered our intelligence to a young fool!'

He was using his cane as a crutch to lift himself up, and he had not yet risen to his fully erect position when his cane slipped out from under his hand. The poor man was not able to maintain his balance. His legs lost their footing, and he fell forward to the floor, landing on his face. Rasūl, who was sitting opposite him, leapt up to break his fall, but to no avail. Rasūl knelt down, turned Sheikh Mālik around, and held his head up in his hands, looking at Abdul-Hamīd and Abdullāh with grave concern. Sheikh Mālik was unconscious and was not moving. Abdul-Hamīd and Abdullāh came over to where Sheikh Mālik and Rasūl were, and the three of them looked at the sheikh, not knowing what to do momentarily. Then Abdul-Hamīd shook Sheikh Mālik and called out to him, but Sheikh Mālik showed no response.

Abdullāh said with concern in his voice, 'His heart... see if his heart is still beating!'

Quicker than Abdul-Hamīd, Rasūl placed his ear on Sheikh Mālik's chest and listened carefully, then said, 'Thank God! He's alive. His heart is beating.'

Abdul-Hamīd said, 'We need to take him to a doctor.'

He looked at Abdullāh and said, 'I'm going to bring the pickup over; you bring him downstairs. We have to go to Nār-Ābād.'

Abdul-Hamīd moved the white curtain aside and hurried down the stairs. Abdullāh looked at Sheikh Mālik with concern and turned to Rasūl and said, 'Help me get him on my shoulders.'

Rasūl and Abdullāh lifted Sheikh Mālik with difficulty and placed him on Abdullāh's shoulders. He was heavier than he looked. He turned to the white curtain at the top of the stairs and said, 'What the hell are we going to do now?!'

Rasūl quickly pulled the curtain aside and Abdullāh made his way down the stairs carefully and arduously. After a moment, Hakīmeh-Khātūn and her mother's voice could be heard speaking excitedly in their native dialect to Abdullāh. Suddenly, the sound of Hakīmeh-Khātūn's mother's wailing could be heard.

Rasūl was now left alone in the room, and he was feeling very concerned. He made his way slowly towards the window and looked outside. It had started to rain. A few people had gathered outside the house. Abdul-Hamīd had backed the pickup to within a few yards of the house, and was helping Abdullāh position Sheikh Mālik into the passenger seat. When one of the women who had gathered around the house saw the state Sheikh Mālik was in, she hit herself on the head with the palms of both hands and let out a loud cry. Rasūl watched them from above, not knowing what to do. He just stood and waited, and no one paid him any mind. Nor was there any news from Hakīmeh-Khātūn or her mother. He sat down and leaned back against the wall. Before too long, he heard a woman's voice say *yā allāh, yā allāh,* and then the white curtain was pulled aside and Hakīmeh-Khātūn's mother entered the room. Rasūl stood up as a sign of respect and greeted her with a *salām,* but Hakīmeh-Khātūn's mother didn't return his *salām.* She stood in front of Rasūl and looked at him very earnestly. Her face was still fully veiled. She spoke very serenely, saying, 'I heard what you had to say, every word of it. If I had any answers to give you, I would have drawn the curtain aside and come into the room like a lion and replied to you, but you saw that I didn't do that.'

Suddenly it was as if a lump had gotten stuck in her throat. She turned away from Rasūl so that he would not see her tears.

'Upon that same Quran that you swore by, your words created a veritable maelstrom in our thoughts and beliefs. Behind the curtain, I hugged Hakīmeh-Khātūn and we wept together. But now that Sheikh Mālik is in this state, there is nothing anyone can do anymore.'

Hakīmeh-Khātūn's mother looked at the window. Taking long strides, she went over and closed it against the rain. Rasūl was looking at the tears that were gathering again in Hakīmeh-Khātūn's mother's eyes. She said with a gentler tone, 'I came to tell you that Sheikh Mālik's words do not represent our thoughts.'

She leaned her head forward and said with a lump in her throat, 'It is the words of the Wahhābi and Salafi extremists. We are Sunnis; we aren't the same as them. Like you, we are afflicted with them and have to deal with them.'

She wiped a tear with the tip of her finger, then continued, 'I do not have the strength to go up against the beliefs of the people of Bīrāh; I can't go up against the ignorance and deviant beliefs of Sheikh Mālik. My children and I must spend a lifetime with these people. You and Hakīmeh-Khātūn are not destined to be with each other. By the right of that same Imam Ali whose love you have in your heart, and by the right of Lady Fātima, the daughter of the

Prophet, leave here and do not come back, and do not mention Hakīmeh-Khātūn's name ever again.'

Hakīmeh-Khātūn's mother lifted the white curtain through her tears and kept it up for Rasūl to pass through. Rasūl stood with a lump in his throat looking at her. He didn't know what to say. He was tongue-tied. He made his way down the stairs. Hakīmeh-Khātūn was nowhere to be seen. Her mother's voice told him, 'Go from the back of the house so that no one will see you. I had your motorcycle moved there.

Rasūl reached the back yard. He stood there, bewildered. The rain came down on his head, and he just stood there, not knowing what to do or where to go. He still didn't understand why everything suddenly went awry and fell apart. He felt tears welling up in his eyes. The pressure of the emotional pain and disappointment he felt made him want to scream. As he stood there in the back yard, the door of a shed stood open, in which he saw his motorcycle. He made his way towards it with slow, measured steps. The rain had soaked all of his clothes. He walked his motorcycle out from the shed, turned it around, and mounted it.

He was thinking of Hakīmeh-Khātūn. He said to himself, *So it's over? Just like that?*

He looked upward, right up to the sky. Rain came down on his cheeks, and on his eyes. Suddenly, from behind him, he heard Hakīmeh-Khātūn call his name.

'Rasūl?'

His whole being shivered. He felt heat course through his whole body. He turned towards the voice and saw Hakīmeh-Khātūn standing in the rain. She looked even more noble and lovable as she stood there in the rain. He wanted to dismount, but there was no life left in his legs. Hakīmeh-Khātūn did not come forward either. She stood at a distance, looking at him. Rasūl could see Hakīmeh-Khātūn's shoulders heaving, and knew that she was weeping bitter tears. They looked at each other, not knowing what to do, utterly bewildered and in silence, under the rain. Looking into each other's eyes, without exchanging a single word.

When the silence was no longer bearable, Rasūl asked through the tears he was trying desperately to hold back, 'Is everything over?'

Hakīmeh-Khātūn nodded.

Rasūl asked, 'For ever?'

Hakīmeh-Khātūn nodded again.

Rasūl could no longer hold back his tears and cried out, his wails filling the back yard.

He asked, 'But *why?!*'

Hakīmeh-Khātūn said, 'I might never see you again.'

The rainclouds rumbled in the dark sky above their heads. Rasūl just looked at Hakīmeh-Khātūn, stunned, weeping now.

Step by step, Hakīmeh-Khātūn slowly approached to within two feet of Rasūl, where she stopped and asked, 'Do you have that prayer set with you? The one with the *turba* (cake of baked clay) made from the clay of Karbalā?'[19]

---

[19] [The event of Āshūrā marks the anniversary of the Battle of Karbalā, when Imam Husayn, the grandson of the Prophet Muhammad, was martyred by the forces of the accursed Umayyad caliph Yazīd in the 61st year of the Islamic calendar or on October 10, 680. The Battle of Karbalā and the Day of

Rasūl nodded. He reached into his jacket pocket and took out the small prayer set wrapped in green velvet and held it out to Hakīmeh-Khātūn. Hakīmeh-Khātūn took it, looked at him and said, 'Can I have it? For always?'

Rasūl nodded. 'For always.'

Rain fell from his hair and cheeks, and his shoulders were shivering from the intensity of his silent weeping.

Hakīmeh-Khātūn looked at him and said, 'Go now.'

Through his tears, Rasūl said, 'For always?'

Hakīmeh-Khātūn nodded her affirmation: 'For always.'

Rasūl switched on his motorcycle and looked at Hakīmeh-Khātūn for the last time. She was standing in the rain like a beautiful angel. He shifted the motorcycle into motion, and sped out of the house's back alley as fast as he could go, and became lost in the barren wilderness. But Hakīmeh-Khātūn too was still in the wilderness, in the backyard of her home. She was standing in the rain, weeping. She slowly opened the green prayer set, took out the *turba* that it contained, kissed it and lowered her forehead onto it. She then replaced the *turba* in its green velvet wrapping, and hid the small prayer set underneath her *chādor*, secreting it away.

The End.

Āshūrā as its focal date, serve as a major element of Shī‘a communal identity.]